To Christopher & Paloma

Best wishes

Maria Symeou

Charlotte
Learns to Forgive

Written by: Maria Symeou

Illustrated by: Joseph Craveiro

Grosvenor House
Publishing Limited

All rights reserved
Copyright © Maria Symeou, 2022

The right of Maria Symeou to be identified as the author of this
work has been asserted in accordance with Section 78
of the Copyright, Designs and Patents Act 1988

The book cover is copyright to Maria Symeou

This book is published by
Grosvenor House Publishing Ltd
Link House
140 The Broadway, Tolworth, Surrey, KT6 7HT.
www.grosvenorhousepublishing.co.uk

This book is sold subject to the conditions that it shall not, by way of
trade or otherwise, be lent, resold, hired out or otherwise circulated
without the author's or publisher's prior consent in any form of binding or
cover other than that in which it is published and
without a similar condition including this condition being imposed
on the subsequent purchaser.

This book is a work of fiction. Any resemblance to
people or events, past or present, is purely coincidental.

A CIP record for this book
is available from the British Library

ISBN 978-1-80381-100-0

My stories are inspired and
dedicated to my children.
Thank you for all your love and support.

Charlotte is a spirited young girl who is creative, competitive, smart, and sporty. She loves exploring nature, planting, enjoys climbing, playing with her friends and she particularly loves animals. She's popular because of her confident, friendly and playful character. She likes to be independent and to make her own decisions – but does she always make the right ones?

Her emotions are provoked, and her thoughts challenged but learning through her mistakes, choices, and everyday life experiences, she starts to understand right from wrong and grows in understanding with each experience she faces in her young life.

Be kind - it's what our parents always tell us. Treat others how you want to be treated. This is the lesson that Charlotte will learn along her journey.

Candy Cane

"I can't reach the candy cane, it's too high up!" said Charlotte, stretching her arm up as far as she could, while standing on the tips of her toes.

"Just wait a moment. I'll come and get it for you, before you pull down the Christmas tree!" said Mum, walking hurriedly towards the living room where the Christmas tree was.

Twelve peppermint candy canes had been put on the tree as part of the Christmas tree decorations. Charlotte could have one candy cane a day. Charlotte loved coming down first thing in the morning and picking a candy cane from the Christmas tree. There was only one left now and she was eager to get it, but Mum had hung it up too high and she couldn't reach it!

"Here's your candy cane but there's no time to start unwrapping and eating it; we're running late. You can eat it later when you get back from school," said Mum.

"Mum, can I please take the candy cane to school with me? I will keep it in my bag and only take it out when school finishes," Charlotte pleaded.

Mum had expected this from Charlotte. "It's better to leave it at home, darling, that way it won't get lost or broken," Mum replied with a smile.

"Now, get your school bag, put your coat and shoes on while I go and get my handbag; we're running late," Mum said, rushing towards the kitchen.

Charlotte was still holding tightly onto the candy cane; she certainly wasn't ready to leave it at home! Quick, she thought, *I'll put it in my bag whilst Mum is still in the kitchen; she'll think I've left it at home.* "I'm ready, Mum," Charlotte said, wanting to distract her mum from any further questions.

"Good, off we go then," Mum said, shutting the front door behind them.

"Tonight, we'll write out Christmas cards for all the children in your class. I'll buy some chocolate coins so you can put one in each of their cards; a little Christmas treat for all your classmates," said Mum.

"Mum, can I put the big chocolate coins in my best friends' cards?" asked Charlotte.

"Yes, Charlotte, you can pick who gets which chocolate coin; after all, that's only fair as you'll be the one writing out all the Christmas cards!" Mum joked.

Mum gave Charlotte a kiss on the cheek and wished her a good day at school. Charlotte said goodbye and walked towards her class.

Now the coast was clear, Charlotte did not hesitate a moment longer. She took out the candy cane from her bag and started to show it to her friends. "Candy cane is my favourite sweet treat but it's my last one," she began to tell her friends.

Miss Lines had spotted Charlotte holding the candy cane and walked over to her. "Charlotte, can you please put the candy cane away in your drawer? Please leave it in there until the end of the day," said Miss Lines. Charlotte hesitated a moment and looked at her candy cane. She liked holding onto it but when Miss Lines said, "Charlotte, I'm waiting," Charlotte knew she had no choice but to put it away in her drawer.

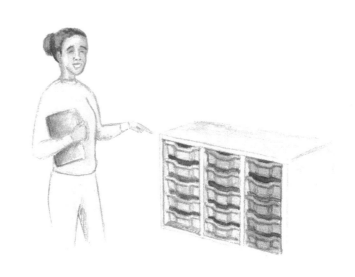

Charlotte did not realise that, during this time, David had been watching her and, more importantly, her candy cane! David had a plan. He was going to wait until all the children finished putting their personal items in their drawers and, when no one was looking, he would go into Charlotte's drawer, open it, and take the prized candy cane!

All the children had settled down and the task given to them was to design a Christmas card. Charlotte had decided to paint a reindeer with antlers and a red nose. She also painted snow falling. She was enjoying her activity so much that she didn't notice David standing by her drawer!

David could hear his heart beating; it was louder and quicker than usual. A rush of excitement and fear came over him at the same time!
He glanced around the classroom one last time to see if anyone was looking or coming towards him. No one had noticed him. This was it! Without hesitating a moment longer, he opened Charlotte's drawer, grabbed the candy cane and quickly shut the drawer again. He took a deep breath and walked away. He was proud that his plan had worked out perfectly. "*I'll have to eat it now, otherwise when Charlotte discovers her candy cane is missing, she'll tell Mrs Lines and they'll start searching everywhere for it. But they won't find it... In my belly!*" he sneakily thought.

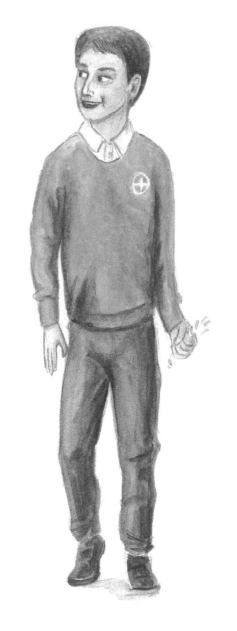

"Miss Lines, can I get my glitter pen from my drawer? I'd like to add some silver sparkly glitter to my card to make it extra special," said Charlotte.

"Yes, that's a great idea, Charlotte, maybe some of the other children might like to add some glitter too," said Miss Lines.

Charlotte walked over to her drawer, whilst humming, *oh Christmas tree, oh Christmas tree, how lovely are your branches*, but suddenly her humming stopped abruptly. "Where's my candy cane?" she yelped.

Nobody heard her the first time; everyone was busy making their Christmas cards, but they sure heard her the next time she shouted, "Where's my candy cane!"

Miss Lines came rushing over to see what had happened. Charlotte had thrown all her belongings from her drawer onto the floor and began opening the other children's drawers, looking for her candy cane. All the children were now looking at her, but no one dared say a word.

"It's not here; someone has taken my candy cane!" Charlotte sobbed.

Miss Lines looked over at all the children. All the children seemed to be where they should be, except... David! "David, what are you doing near the book corner?" asked Miss Lines. David could feel his cheeks going red and he stopped chewing the last bit of the candy cane that was still in his mouth. "David, can you please come over here?" requested Miss Lines.

David slowly walked over to Miss Lines. He was trying to finish off the last bit of candy cane, but it was too late. "Stop chewing!" said Miss Lines in a firm tone. David did as he was told. "David, can you tell me what you are chewing?" asked Miss Lines. David remained silent. "Open your mouth and stick your tongue out," continued Miss Lines. Some of the children gasped at what Miss Lines had just asked David to do.

Oh no, I'm in big trouble, thought David. He hesitated for a moment, but Miss Lines would not take her eyes off him; she was waiting for him to open his mouth! He took one last gulp, opened his mouth, and stuck out his tongue.

"Argh!" screeched Charlotte as she saw the chewed-up red, white and green candy cane on his tongue.

"David Johnson, go to the book corner immediately. I will speak with you in just a moment. This behaviour is unacceptable!" David did not say a word; he put his head down and walked over to the book corner.

"I hate him, he's ruined everything!"
Charlotte shouted, throwing her glitter
pen to the floor.

Miss Lines tried to comfort her, telling her,
"Don't worry I'm sure there's more candy
at home for you." That upset Charlotte even
more as it reminded her it was her last
candy cane! Miss Lines gave her a tissue to
wipe away her tears. "Now let's put your
belongings back in your drawer and go and finish off
your special Christmas card," she said softly. Charlotte
finally stopped crying but she was not in a good mood.
She just wanted Mum to come and take her home.

Miss Lines went to speak with David. She told him children who take other children's belongings, must think about their mistake and the consequences of their action. In David's case, he missed out on the Christmas card activity and was not allowed any outdoor playtime either. Charlotte got through the day, but she did not talk much. She was still incredibly angry with David. How could he do such a thing?

It was finally time to go home. Charlotte could see her mum waiting outside her classroom. *What will Mum say about David eating my candy cane?* she thought. *Mum will be upset with me because I didn't listen to her when she told me to leave it at home, but I have to tell her the truth, because Mum always makes me feel better when I'm upset and feeling sad.*

Miss Lines called Charlotte's mum in for a quiet word. When Mum finished speaking with Miss Lines, she turned to Charlotte with a smile and said, "Come on, young lady, let's go home." Charlotte remained quiet but held tightly onto Mum's hand. She felt comforted holding Mum's hand. "Charlotte, tell me what happened at school today," Mum said.

"Well, I'm very upset and I hate David!" blurted out Charlotte.

"That does not sound good. Why do you hate David? Tell me what happened," asked Mum.

"He stole my candy cane and went and hid and ate it all up!" replied Charlotte with a huff.

"Hmm, I see. Is this the same candy cane that I asked you to leave at home, by any chance? When I give you advice or ask you to do something, it's because I want to protect you or keep you safe, or even stop someone eating your candy, do you understand?"

Charlotte looked at Mum and nodded. She realised that Mum's advice was right. "I'm sorry, Mummy, I should have listened to you. I just wanted to take it with me and look forward to eating it after school, but it's gone. That horrible David has eaten it and it's in his belly, not mine!" said Charlotte in a cross voice.

"Charlotte, do you remember what I said I would buy today?" Mum said, wanting to distract Charlotte.

"Erm…" Charlotte thought for a moment. "Chocolate coins!" she shouted out loudly.

"Yes, excellent memory! Here I have some gold and silver chocolate coins, and a list of the children's names Miss Lines gave to me. When we get home you can start writing out Christmas cards," Mum said.

"I know, I'll give the silver ones to the boys and gold ones to the girls," said Charlotte, feeling happy with her decision.

Charlotte was happy to be back home. She had a cheese and cucumber sandwich to keep her going until dinner. She opened the bags with chocolate coins and helped herself to one. "Mum, I'm ready to start writing out Christmas cards," Charlotte said.

"Here's the list of names. Tick off their name once you have written out their card. You'll need to write: 'To...', then add the child's name and sign it off 'from Charlotte'. Got it?" asked Mum.

"Yes, Mum, and not to forget the chocolate coins, either!" replied Charlotte.

She was halfway down the list when she came across David's name. "No way, he's not getting a Christmas card and chocolate coin from me, I hate him!" Charlotte said boldly.

Aaron ☑
Amy ☑
Adam ☑
Bobby ☑
Chloë ☑
David ☐

"Charlotte," said Mum. Charlotte looked at Mum and Mum continued. "Remember, you too made a wrong choice when you took the candy cane into school today - when I'd asked you not to. So, when you make a wrong choice or make a mistake - which upsets me, how would you feel if I didn't forgive you? ...or give you another chance to at least make it right again?"

"I would be sad because that would make me think you didn't love me anymore," replied Charlotte thoughtfully.

"Do you now see how important it is to forgive one another? It shows the other person you haven't stopped loving or caring for them, you're giving them another chance to make it right again and, hopefully, they will learn from their mistake. Remember, if you want to be forgiven when you make mistakes or wrong choices, should you not also forgive others for theirs?" asked Mum.

Charlotte hesitated for a moment, then looked back at Mum and said, "Okay, I will write him out a Christmas card and I will put a chocolate coin in the card, but a small one, though," Charlotte said.

"But can you imagine how he will feel if you gave him a big chocolate coin? He will be so happy to know that you still care and have forgiven him," said Mum.

With slight hesitation, and with a sigh, Charlotte said, "Alright, Mum, I will, but I hope he learns never to eat my candy cane again!

The next morning, Charlotte was excited to hand out the Christmas cards. She started to hand them out while the children were waiting to go into their class. Each child would come to Charlotte and she would give them their card. The children were extremely excited to discover a chocolate coin in their card. David saw the other children getting a Christmas card and a chocolate coin. He thought to himself, *I won't be getting a Christmas card from Charlotte; she hates me!*

Charlotte's mum spotted David and said to Charlotte, "David is over there, I think he is waiting for you to call him over."

Charlotte looked towards David's direction and caught his eye. She signalled for him to come over. David did not hesitate a moment longer and rushed over. Charlotte handed him over his Christmas card. Before David even opened the card, he leaped forward and gave Charlotte a huge hug and said with the happiest voice, "Thank you so much, Charlotte!"

Both Mum and Charlotte were surprised by David's reaction. Charlotte was lost for words; she didn't expect David to be so grateful for the Christmas card, and he hadn't even discovered the big chocolate coin yet!

Mum smiled at them both and when David walked away, she whispered to Charlotte, "David was the most grateful out of all the children who received a Christmas card from you today; do you know why that is?"

"I think it's because I forgave him, Mummy," said Charlotte.

"Yes, Charlotte, you forgave him. David knows you still care about him because you're giving him another chance. You see, forgiving and being kind to one another is such a wonderful gift," said Mum.

"Yes, and it's not just for Christmas!" said Charlotte, smiling back at Mum.

A little bit about the author...

Maria Symeou lives in Hertfordshire with her two children and four laying hens. She started writing children's stories after realising how much her captive, young audience enjoyed her storytelling.

Inspired by her children and hoping to teach them some important life-values, she began work writing the Charlotte Learning Collection.

When not writing, Maria enjoys entertaining family and friends - any excuse to eat, drink and laugh!

And the illustrator...

Joseph is a freelance artist who lives in Essex. After studying product design in Brunel University, he worked as a freelance graphic designer, but has now started a new career path following his passion for art, in illustration.

Joseph has worked with Maria to bring her storytelling to life with colourful imagery to help spread the important life-values included in the stories.

Lightning Source UK Ltd.
Milton Keynes UK
UKHW052119141122
412187UK00009B/226